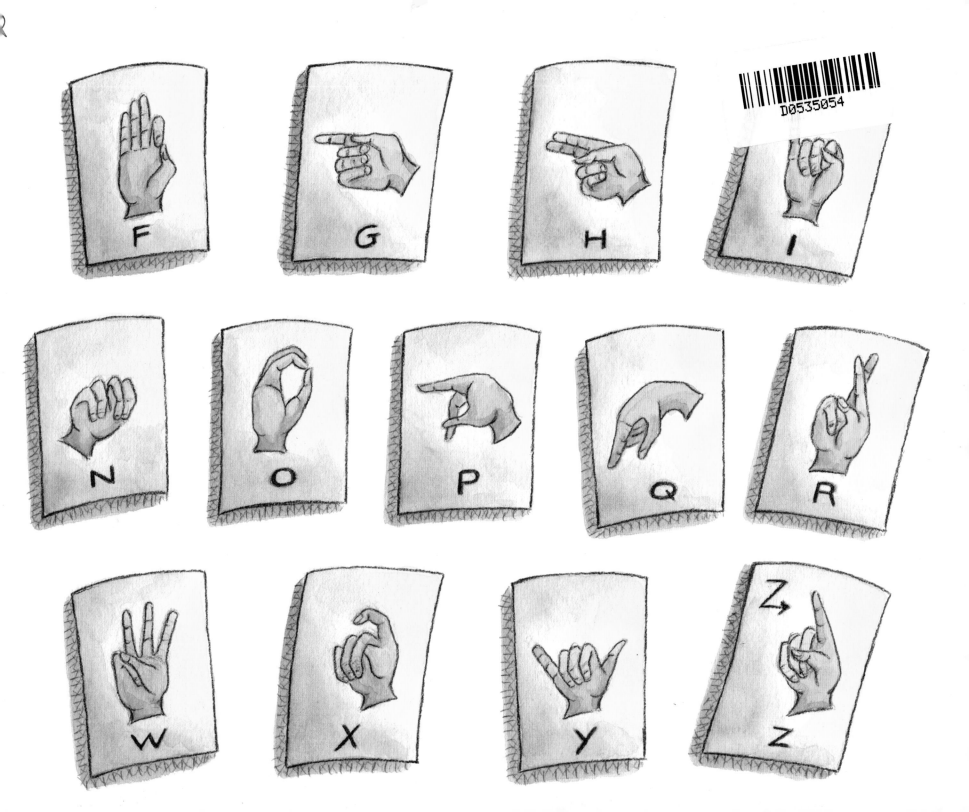

Helen Keller's Best Friend Belle

Holly M. Barry

Illustrated by
Jennifer Thermes

Albert Whitman & Company
Chicago, Illinois

To my mom and dad for all of their encouragement, with love —*H.M.B.*

For Allison, my mom. Your compassion inspires. —*J.T.*

Library of Congress Cataloging-in-Publication data is on file with the publisher.

Text copyright © 2013 by Holly M. Barry
Illustrations © 2013 by Jennifer Thermes
Published in 2013 by Albert Whitman & Company.
ISBN 978-0-8075-3198-3

Printed in China.
10 9 8 7 6 5 4 3 2 1 BP 18 17 16 15 14 13

The design is by Nick Tiemersma.

For more information about Albert Whitman & Company,
visit our web site at www.albertwhitman.com.

 Helen Keller was born on a farm called Ivy Green in Tuscumbia, Alabama, on June 27, 1880. She was a bright and beautiful baby. She started talking when she was six months old. By her first birthday she could walk.

But six months later, Helen became very sick with a high fever. It caused her to lose her sight and hearing. Helen's world became quiet and dark.

She could no longer talk to her parents. She forgot the words she had learned. Helen didn't know how to explain what she was thinking and feeling. She felt alone and afraid.

Often, the only ones who could comfort Helen were her dogs. They were patient, gentle, and affectionate.

It didn't matter that she couldn't see, hear, or talk to them. Whenever she reached out to touch them, they were always close beside her. Helen's dogs became her devoted companions.

When Helen was six years old, she had an old setter named Belle. Helen followed her everywhere.

Belle was beside Helen on the most important day of her life.

On March 3, 1887, Anne Sullivan came to Alabama to
live with Helen and her family. Anne was a teacher from
the Perkins School for the Blind. She came to help Helen
and open up a whole new world for her.

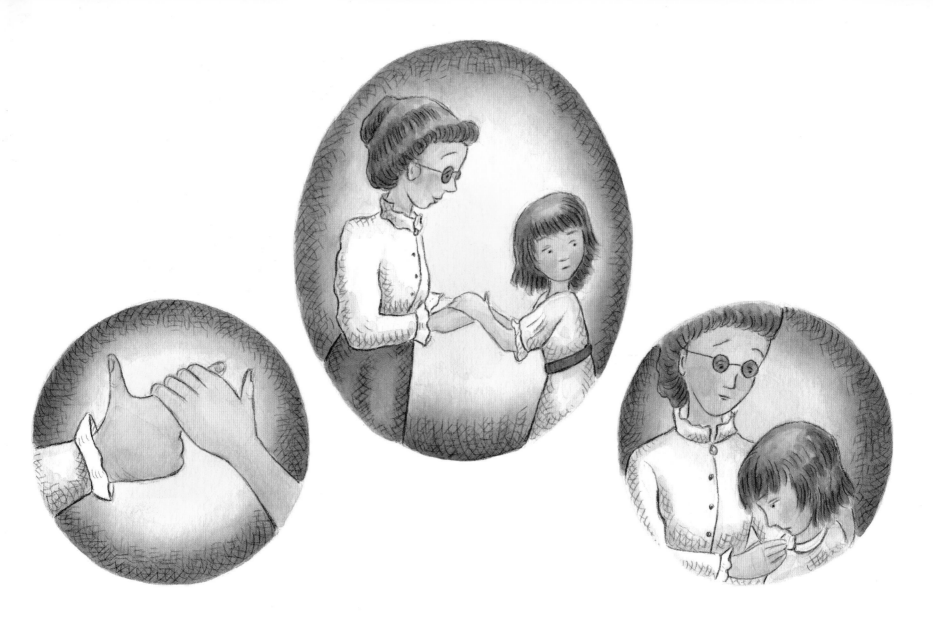

Anne taught Helen how to communicate
by using finger spelling in the palm of her
hand. At first Helen did not understand
the meaning of the words.

Anne gave Helen a doll
and spelled *d-o-l-l*.
She gave her a hat
and spelled *h-a-t*.

Helen thought it was a game.

One day Anne held Helen's hand under the water flowing
from a pump. She spelled *w-a-t-e-r* in her palm.

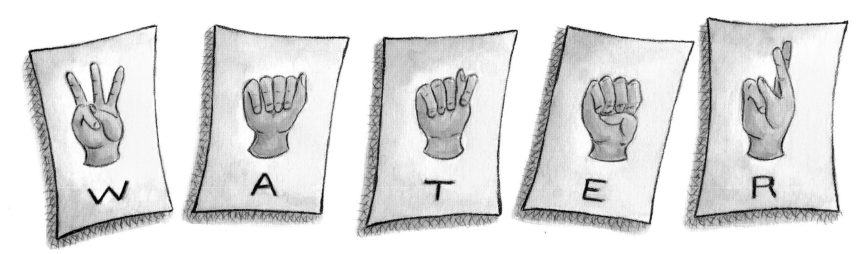

At last Helen understood that water was something cool that she could feel running down on her hand. For Helen, making the connection was electric!

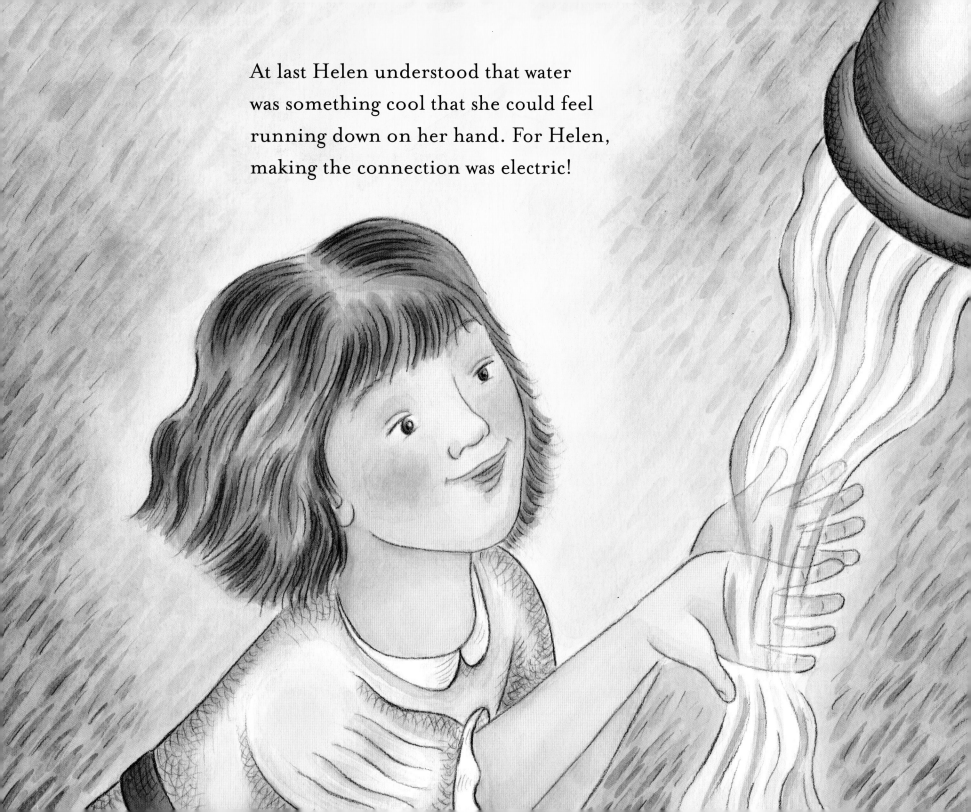

The moment Helen learned that first word, her world went from darkness into the light. She learned thirty words that day.

She tried to teach Belle how to spell in her small paw. Belle didn't understand what Helen was doing, but she liked the attention. Belle sat still and wagged her tail while Helen practiced spelling all her new words.

Many of Helen's lessons were outside. She and Anne took long walks in the woods with Belle. Anne encouraged Helen to explore and discover things on her own.

One morning Helen came running upstairs to find
Anne. She was filled with excitement. Helen spelled
"dog-baby" and then held up her five fingers. Anne
did not understand what Helen was trying to tell her.

Helen took Anne's hand and led her outside. There in the
back of the house was a mother dog with her five tiny pups!

Anne taught Helen the word *puppy* while Helen touched the dogs' soft fur. Helen pointed to each puppy, and Anne spelled "five puppies."

One pup was smaller than the others. Helen held the pup and spelled "small." Anne then spelled "very small." Helen laughed when the puppies started to squirm and she played with them for the rest of the afternoon.

Once Helen knew thousands of words, Anne taught her to use Braille, a form of writing for the blind. Braille uses patterns of raised dots that represent numbers and letters in the alphabet.

Helen learned to read by feeling the words with her fingertips.

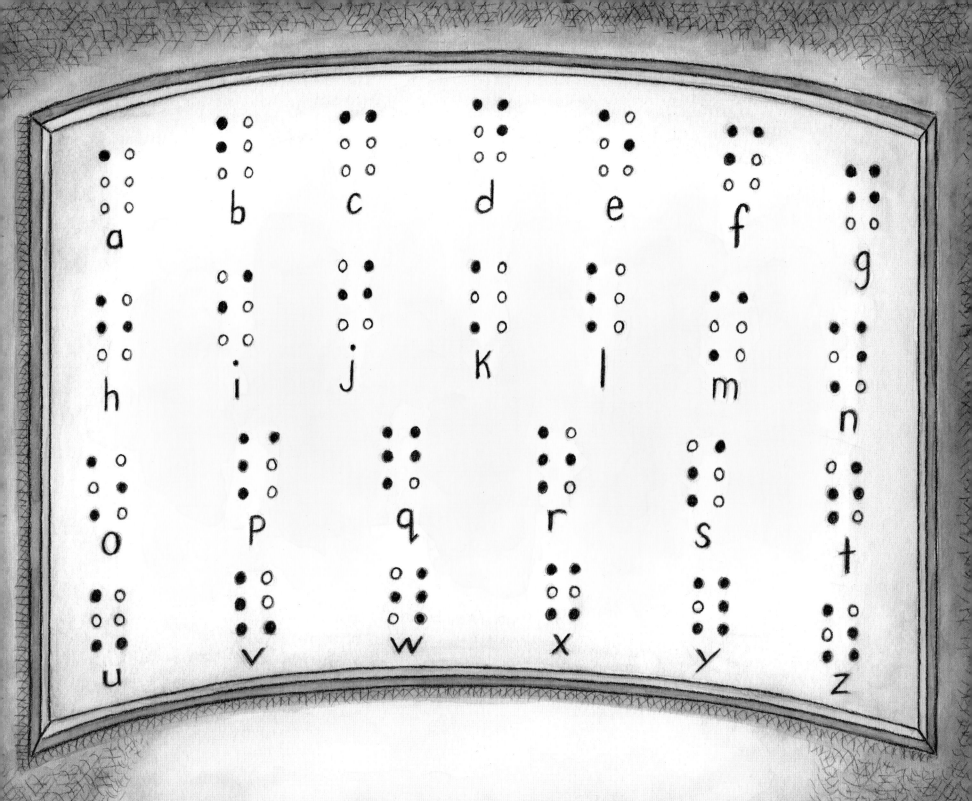

When Helen was ten years old, she wanted to learn how to speak with her voice so everyone could understand her.

Anne took Helen to Boston in the spring of 1890 to meet Miss Sarah Fuller. She was the principal at the Horace Mann School for the Deaf.

Miss Fuller tried to teach Helen to speak using her voice. Helen would lightly feel Miss Fuller's mouth when she spoke. Then Helen tried to repeat the words. It was hard for Helen because she couldn't hear the sounds or see her teacher's mouth.

After many hours of practicing,
Helen said her first sentence:
"It is warm."

When Anne and Helen came home, they were greeted by her mother, father, and little sister, Mildred.

Helen called out to her dog, "Come, Belle!" Belle came running to Helen and licked her hand. In that moment Helen was filled with joy. Now Belle could understand her too!

Helen had a lifelong love of dogs. When she was a child, her family owned Irish and English setters. Helen's favorite was an Irish setter named Belle. In *The Story of My Life*, Helen wrote that Belle was her constant companion and she tried hard to teach the dog to spell. Anne Sullivan noticed Helen's affection for dogs as well. Two months after she arrived in Alabama, Anne wrote a letter to her friend describing Helen's delight in discovering a litter of puppies.

Years later at Radcliffe College, Helen's classmates gave her a Boston terrier as a reward for completing her midterm exams. Helen loved the dog and named him Phiz.

In 1937, when Helen was on a speaking tour in Japan, she admired an Akita, a Japanese dog breed. The Akita's owner gave her one as a gift. The dog was named Kamikaze-Go and Helen was the first person to bring an Akita to the United States.

Kamikaze-Go was soon joined by his brother, Kenzan-Go, and both dogs held a very special place in Helen's heart.

Throughout her life, Helen had Great Danes, a mastiff, German shepherds, Shetland collies, Irish and English setters, springer spaniels, a Boston terrier, bull terriers, Akitas, Scottish terriers, dachshunds, and a variety of mixed breeds. Helen was photographed many times with her beloved companions.

Helen cherished her dogs for their unconditional love, loyalty, and companionship. They gave her a lifetime of happiness. She said in her autobiography, "My dog friends seem to understand my limitations, and always keep close beside me when I am alone. I love their affectionate ways and eloquent wag of their tales. Their warm, tender, and playful friendships are so comforting to me."

Helen Keller was born on June 27, 1880, in Tuscumbia, Alabama. When Helen was nineteen months old, an illness left her blind and deaf. With the help of her teacher Anne Sullivan, Helen became an author, lecturer, and advocate for people with disabilities.

In 1900, Helen attended Radcliffe College in Cambridge, Massachusetts. During classes Anne spelled everything the teachers said into Helen's hand. While in college, Helen wrote her autobiography, *The Story of My Life*. It was published in 1903 and sold around the world. A year later, Helen graduated with honors. She was the first deaf and blind person to write a book and earn a degree from college.

Helen began a career of writing and lecturing about her life. She and Anne traveled around the country giving speeches on how to educate deaf and blind children. Helen courageously worked to get them better schools and libraries.

After Anne died in 1936, Helen continued to travel with a companion, visiting 39 countries to raise awareness and money for people with disabilities. She worked for their rights to have a better education, more responsibilities, and opportunities for employment. Helen worked for the American Foundation for the Blind for more than 40 years as well. She received many awards for her service. In 1964, President Lyndon Johnson presented her with the Presidential Medal of Freedom, the highest honor that an American civilian can receive.

Helen worked until she was 81 years old. Six years later, on June 1, 1968, she died peacefully in her sleep. Helen was a remarkable woman who devoted her life to helping those in need. She is an inspiration to millions of people.